VIKING KESTREL

Distributed by the Penguin Group
27 Wrights Lane, London W8 5TZ, England
Viking Penguin Inc., 40 West 23rd Street, New York, New York 10010, USA
Penguin Books Australia Ltd, Ringwood, Victoria, Australia
Penguin Books Canada Ltd, 2801 John Street, Markham, Ontario, Canada L3R 1B4
Penguin Books (NZ) Ltd, 182–190 Wairau Road, Auckland 10, New Zealand

Penguin Books Ltd, Registered Offices: Harmondsworth, Middlesex, England

First American edition 1990

Typeset in Univers
Printed by L.E.G.O. Vicenza

ISBN 0–670–83074–7

All Gone!

SARAH GARLAND

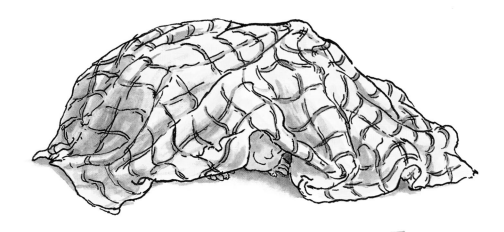

xz
004

VIKING KESTREL

Teddy bear

All gone!

Yellow nightie

All gone!

Boiled egg

All gone!

Ten toes

All gone!

Our cat

All gone!

Big bone

All gone!

Red balloon

All gone!

Blue car

All gone!

21

Cat's dinner

All gone!

Drink of milk

All gone!

Bath water

All gone!

Story book

All gone!